PUDDLES

By Jonathan London
Pictures by G. Brian Karas

PUFFIN BOOKS

For Sean and Max and Marc—puddle-jumpers!

PUFFIN BOOKS
Published by the Penguin Group
Penguin Putnam Books for Young Readers, 345 Hudson Street, New York, New York 10014, U.S.A.
Penguin Books Ltd, 27 Wrights Lane, London W8 5TZ, England
Penguin Books Australia Ltd, Ringwood, Victoria, Australia
Penguin Books Canada Ltd, 10 Alcorn Avenue, Toronto, Ontario, Canada M4V 3B2
Penguin Books (N.Z.) Ltd, 182-190 Wairau Road, Auckland 10, New Zealand

Penguin Books Ltd, Registered Offices: Harmondsworth, Middlesex, England

First published in the United States of America by Viking,
a division of Penguin Books USA Inc., 1997
Published by Puffin Books, a member of Penguin Putnam Books for Young Readers, 1999

3 5 7 9 10 8 6 4 2

THE LIBRARY OF CONGRESS HAS CATALOGED THE VIKING EDITION AS FOLLOWS:
London, Jonathan.
Puddles / by Jonathan London ; pictures by G. Brian Karas.
p. cm.
Summary: When the rain stops falling and the skies clear up, it's time
to put on boots and go outside to play in the puddles.
ISBN 0-670-87218-0 (hc.)
[1. Rain and rainfall—Fiction.] I. Karas, G. Brian, ill. II. Title.
PZ7.L8432Pu 1997 [E]—dc21 96-52794 CIP AC

Puffin Books ISBN 0-14-056175-7

Printed in Hong Kong

All night the slash
of rain and the flash
of lightning, and the

Ka-**BOOM!**

of thunder rattling
the house and all
the windows. We cuddle
between fright
and glee and want it
to stop
and never stop.

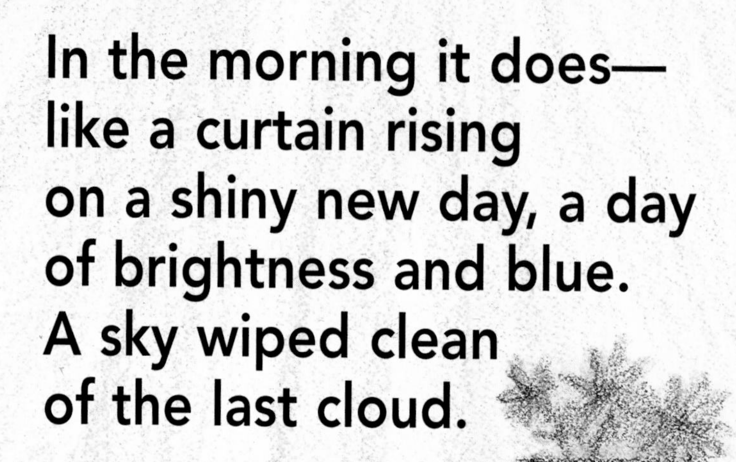

In the morning it does—
like a curtain rising
on a shiny new day, a day
of brightness and blue.
A sky wiped clean
of the last cloud.

We walk outside
to the sweet chatter
of birds
filling the trees
and breathe deep the clear air.

"Watch out for puddles!" Mama hollers.
"Don't get wet!"

Needles glisten—
listen—
the *drip* *drip* *drip*
from the eaves
and the leaves.
Look—the sparkle
of a million suns
in a million drops!

We follow baby rivers
trickling and snaking
down ditches into fields.

Puddles! Big ones, little ones,
long ones, skinny ones—
pieces of sky
on the ground.
It's time to puddle-jump!
Splash splash splash!

Mud sucks
at our boots—*slup slup slup.*

We kneel and watch worms squirm
and stretch and leave tiny trails
in the muck like sloppy writing—
they're learning the ABCs
of weather, of rain and sun and mud.

Then we slog down through wet grass
toward the pond and what
lives there, celebrating
all the new water and new life.

At the pond, it's time for the frogs to play! And we want to play with them. *Leap frog, leap!*
Leap frog, leap!
Hop, flop—*plop!*

Birds flap
from the trees
and we think the trees
are applauding!
We bow, then say, "Bye, frogs!"
and turn toward home.

Puddles! Big ones, little ones,
long ones, skinny ones—
pieces of sky
on the ground.
It's time to puddle-jump again!
We can hit every puddle
from the pond to the meadow—
splash splash splash!

We slog through wet grass
and suck mud with our boots—
slup slup slup

skip beneath leaves and eaves—
drip drip drip

and drip in the doorway shouting,
"We're home!"
"You're *wet!*" Mama howls.

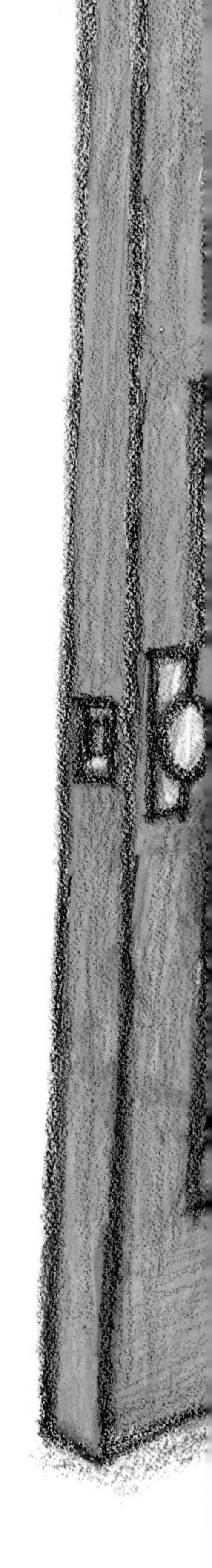

On a morning after rain
it's time to soak in a hot bath . . .
wiggle dry in a warm towel . . .

get dressed and drink hot chocolate . . .

then run outside again

to puddle-jump—*splash splash splash!*